THE
COAST
OF
NOWHERE

The Coast of Nowhere

*Meditations on rivers,
lakes and streams*

Michael Delp

 Wayne State University Press · Detroit

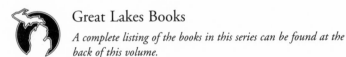

Great Lakes Books

A complete listing of the books in this series can be found at the back of this volume.

Philip P. Mason, Editor
Department of History, Wayne State University

Dr. Charles K. Hyde, Associate Editor
Department of History, Wayne State University

Manufactured in the United States of America.

01 00 99 98   5 4 3 2

Library of Congress Cataloging in Publication Data

Delp, Michael.
    The coast of nowhere : mediations on rivers, lakes and streams / Michael Delp.
        p.   cm. -- (Great Lakes Books)
    ISBN 0-8143-2711-7 (pbk: alk. paper)
    1. Rivers--Literary collections.   2. Lakes--Literary collections.
3. Meditations.   I. Title   II. Series.
PS3554.E44447C63   1997
818'.5409--dc21   97-20632

Some of this work has appeared in *Passages North, Traverse the Magazine, Prime Time, The Riverwatch,* and the *Patagonia Catalog.*

In Memory of
Dave Lemmen

Contents

What It Is   *11*

I. THE TEXT OF THE RIVER

The Text of the River   *17*

Riverdog   *23*

Fishing the Winter River   *27*

Walking the River, December   *34*

Middle Distance: The Balm of Water   *37*

Winter: Dancing at
    the Edge of Nothing   *40*

Following the Pull in the Blood   *43*

Dawn Streamers   *45*

King of the Brook Trout   *47*

II. INTO THE BLACK RIVER

River Ghazals   *55*

III. THE DREAM RIVERS

The River Inside   *73*

The Dream Rivers   *81*

The River Everywhere   *88*

IV. INTO THE BACK COUNTRY

Last Pool   *97*

The Coast of Nowhere   *101*

What My Father Told Me   *103*

A Daughter's Preface

My father's soul is made of water; river water that silver
trout swim through and old fishermen love. It's always
been a mystery to me, people's souls. You can't see them,
but my father's soul is more clear to me than most things
in this world. I know that if I could hold it in my small
hand, I would be holding poetry and rivers and thoughts.
Then, in the deep shadows, I would find a tiny trout fly
that holds it all together.

Jaime Delp

What It Is

a fly-fishing manifesto

WHAT IT IS, IS THIS: after decades of fishing you come to realize that you live in a house made entirely of desire. Everything is fishing, a life given over to the obsession to be on the water, a way water has of leaking into every pore, every synapse, every fissure of bone, your marrow gone liquid. At night you hear the fly line singing, and that's exactly what it is, singing, in the living room, the line moving rhythmically past the chairs, curving around the television as if it were a river boulder, the fish holding just under the surface of the tube.

The stairs are water, falling water, the runs and pools threaded into the risers, the places where your feet have taken you to dreams for all these years. There is water running in the house, rivers coursing in the copper lines, and the deep well, always a conduit to that other place, the dark place where fear and longing sit like twin brothers waiting to slip up into the light, make themselves known, carry their rods to the rivers you dream each night.

In the morning, a glass of water surges from the tap and you drink the very bodies of fish into your own body. You stand in the first light glinting off the river, light which moves in streams through the windows and your entire body shifts to fit that light, the light moving past you like water. Then the transformation, the movement of light through your eyes and into your veins and you want to gather up your rods and reels, the vest and flies, leave the house and dissolve away.

What it is, is your body becoming like the rivers you fish. The gravel bars and flats inside your body, each memory of fishing in the rain etched topographically until your heart is one solid piece of river terrain. You dream that your heart has its own desires: that it can call you in, and that when you enter the heart chambers, the map of every river you've ever fished rolls out under your feet, the landscape falling like rain into place; the desire to fish always on your lips, each word marked by the sound of moving water, the river in each fleck of your eyes.

What it is, is to know that the rivers are haunted. That someday your father will be on the river exactly where he said he'd meet you. Your grandfather will be there too, and the dead friends who gave you their desire to fish like a man hands over a chalice to the man he leaves behind. All their graves will be empty.

What it is, is to know the air and the sky, the trees, the smallest places where water rests and eddies, then eventually travels on. How the sky is more mirror than anything else and that with even more desire you could fish the clouds, the sky moving past greater than any river.

What it is, is to know a way inside. That your mind travels down the line, through the fly, past the hook into the water and back through your feet, entering your head cleaner, wider, the river a thread, a rope, a knotless strand of silk.

Back at the house it is still desire in the rooms, desire rising in your wife, and daughter, the way their eyes flash, the retinas moist, wet, a thin film of water between you and what they see in you. What it is, is to lift them up and take them outside, tell them to lean close to your chest and listen: a heart running to catch up with the cataracts it creates.

What it is, is to know that you die going in, you die going under and you die on the bottom. But your body stays there, then sifts away. They won't find you. They will search for days, find your rod, your hat maybe, even a piece of the sandwich you didn't finish, a half empty shot of whiskey in the deep bend you named after your daughter. They will grieve and wait there on the shore for days, weeks, standing in all kinds of weather and they will leave flowers for you, trinkets, messages written on birch bark. They will call up and down the river and some of them may see your ghost in the cedars. They will think you have gone for good, that you have taken up residence in a place marked by wild rivers, wild fish, a place only dreamed of. But what it is, finally, is to know that your heart is water itself. Always has been. But they will come to that slowly, when they wake at night in the house and hear the ghost line humming over their heads and feel something wild and pulsing, surging in their own hearts.

PART 1

THE TEXT OF THE RIVER

The Text of the River

1

YOUR BLOOD TELLS YOU FIRST. Maybe on a warm night in May, your blood changes its course, comes from somewhere beyond your body, from the ground, or from that spring you first saw years ago in the woods. Water coming from an iron ring in a small clearing, and you looked . . . first in and then down into a perfect dark circle of water like an eye, a dark pupil, and you feel this water entering your legs first, then sifting upward into your heart.

Now, you realize you've carried this river in your heart for years. The slight taste of iron, the smell of the underbelly of ten thousand years while the glacier moved down, traced the course of that other river, and now this river is inside you.

Call it memory, call it the way your hands cup the water to drink, call it the form your life has taken, how what you do each day shapes itself around the river in your heart, or call it by name. . . AuSable, River of Sand . . . and know that your pulse rides on the back of water, rides for miles through swamps and deadfall, and know that the words you speak come from the mouth of the river, that even your skin, your hair, your face, has river in it.

To get to the river all you need is to sit still, drop down, let your body remember the way the river moves: always by way of gradient, a falling from higher to lower, a way your body has of lengthening out, thinking itself loose in the river. Not as water, but as the way time might mix with water, in swirls, in small whirlpools, or in the long runs of riffles dropping into deep pools. And it never stops but keeps running, falling, moving, your life sifted and re-sifted, as though you were once whole, a man, flesh and blood. And now you begin to understand the thin film of river which holds you together. A life gone over to water, a river, each movement in your life a part of losing yourself, getting yourself back, your heart always lifting water from that first deep spring.

2

Deep in the heart, deeper than memory, deeper
than any water, under the river, in the grey rain of
another kind of sky, the god of fish spends his days
pulling the new grey bodies of fish from his side. He
brings them to his lips, infuses them with the colors
he senses inside him, bright silvers, slight touches of
blue, some of them full pinks, their backs dotted like
rain, then raises them upward into the world, speaking their names: brook trout, brown, rainbow. He
tells them that death is the water they part, that the
river will hold them, take them home, into the heart
once more; in my pulse, in the wash of my memory,
in the dance of the river, in my own clear eyes.

3

How do I speak the name of gravel, the heart of water? How do I walk the river for miles and never lose myself? How do I let my body fall into the river and not turn away from the world? How do I sift the river for voices? How do I rise each day and smell the odor of cedar in my skin? How will I follow this river if the river is inside me? Where do I find the dark lips of the river to offer the ragged edges of my life for healing?

4

Rain to earth, a single cut along my arm. Blood drains into the river, the blood of memory, of loss, of fear and desire, gone downstream. What seeps in is wild, part fish, part plant, the real blood of gods who still live, gods who are rivers themselves, gods who move like water over the surface of my heart, gods who move beside you in the rivers you fish, the gods of rivers who come into the body riding the flesh of brook trout, and the intoxicant single god of the one true river where you give blood and take blood. This is the god who bleeds into you, who stands up every day and makes you move through your life, remembering rain, sleet, snow, the way each form of water falls, mixes, passes away.

5

I walk the till of the glacier: sand, gravel, silt, clay
and stones, moving up sometimes into the hilly
moraines where the ice front stood still. There are
times when months pass, then I wake to the sound
of ice melting, and hear again the way the river
leaves behind what it means. I carry the stones of
ten thousand years home, lay them down on the
desk, sort and re-sort. I roll them in my fingers like
dice, let them fall again and again, reading the pattern each time looking for some kind of omen, a
prophecy, reading them like braille, like religion.

Riverdog

What you need is to get over here on the river
and live like a dog.

—Dave Lemmen

In July of 1949, six months after my baptism, my grandfather carried me into the water of Bass Lake. As my mother tells it, he knelt there in the darkness and filtered palms of lake water over my legs, motioning with his hands toward islands, drop-offs and his best fishing spots. For years I drifted the lake with him and my father, casting our plugs toward shore, the Bible music from Camp Concordia countering our low whispers for the fish gods to send us luck. Later, in my teens, after the cottage sold, I cruised town with my buddies, the notions of water seemingly unimportant when compared with the bodies of cheerleaders and the grail of beer.

Twenty-one years later and newly married, I headed north to teach and live in Northern Michigan. Looking back, I know that juncture, that place where my life could have gone anywhere, took a defining turn toward a life on the water. I grew up a lake boy, but was always looking toward brushy creeks and farm streams hoping to see a glimpse of a brook trout, not content with catching bass and panfish. I wanted trout, wanted to enter that vaulted world of fly-fishing, wicker creels and bamboo rods. What I sense now, in my mid-forties, is that what I really wanted was to always be in the presence of rivers. I wanted to become a riverdog, smelling of cedar swamps, river mud, my face lined from month after month of living on the water.

I am convinced now, after spending a good many days on trout streams, that rivers come from the veins of the gods themselves. Surely, rivers are the blood of the beings more capable and sensible than we are and to stand waist deep in a trout stream is to make contact with the pure spirit of the gods themselves. Not true of lakes, literal bowls of water lodged in the earth.

Through turns of fate, I have lived on lakes for years and find them fairly uninteresting in their containment when compared to the coursing motion of the moving water of rivers. If a man can "seldom be appeased by house current after he has been hit by lightning," then my life spent on lakes is the equivalent of sucking on a couple of "D" cells. True, I have watched lakes for hours, heaving and churning in storms, but there is always the idea that the water never leaves. Put your soul afloat on a lake and you'll likely get it back. Do the same on a river and you'll be able to let yourself drift away for good.

The movement of rivers is fundamental to their power for me. Learning a river is a textual process.

Go to a river as you would a text and you'll likely learn far more than attending a lifetime of cocktail parties, sales meetings, task force initiatives or MFA courses. On a given trout stream there are thousands of bits of information constantly changing and rearranging themselves; the movements of fish hidden under the surface, the face of the river always offering up a mirror of the sky.

Even more powerful for me is the notion that being in a river has something to do with the process of letting the crush of the world sift out of you. Countless times I have let go of cars that won't start, mountains of debt, the bitter taste of arguments. Each time the river takes the debris of my life away. And when I turn to look upstream, there is almost always something floating down to me that I thought I had lost forever. I have seen the ghosts of ancestors along the river and I have seen myself standing under the shade of sweeping cedars, always the words of admonition coming from my ghost mouth to cash it in and give myself over to water.

Lately, I've been fantasizing about doing just that. I'm haunted by an old photograph from the late 1800s of a salmon king on the Colombia River. Once a year, the chief would don a ceremonial suit made entirely of salmon skins, his arms stretching over the water calling to the sky for a bountiful harvest of fish.

In my waking dreams I see myself standing in the doorway of a ramshackle cabin, the deep light of an October afternoon glinting off the scales of my brook trout skin shirt. I'd long since have changed my name to Muddler or Matuka and would have risen each day to a breakfast of fresh brook trout. My eyes would see clearly once more, surely I could see in all directions, the trout in me looking up at the moon, a milky disk, even farther from the world of men.

Fishing the Winter River

There are no tracks down to the river. Not any human tracks anyway. The woods have that stillness they hold all winter: in this relatively warm winter air sound is muffled enough so that when you speak a word, perhaps your own name, it hangs only inches from your mouth then dies quickly. In colder weather I have heard traffic from M–72, three miles away, sounding as if it were on top of me.

My second thought isn't of the weighted nymphs I'll use or how heavy a tippet to fish for a perfect dead drift. I think of June. Late June and this same stretch of water alive with Brown Drakes. I've fished where I'm standing so many times I know I could fish it blind. I fished a score of Sunday mornings up under the sweeping arms of cedars, streamers before dawn. I aimed for the dark pools, the browns looking for one more brook trout before the sun cracked the tree line. And one particular day in mid-August when it was almost a hundred degrees and no air. I left a friend's cabin, sweating profusely in the twenty steps down to the river then cast lackadaisically to no fish until I put a grasshopper up under a hanging cedar, dropping it just at the mouth of a small feeder creek. What followed was fifteen minutes of thrashing around in the heat with an eighteen-inch rainbow. Dead luck. Dead hot.

But today, of course, I feel the cold even in my teeth. I feel like something dressed not for this world but for a Martian night, moving stiffly like a kid bundled up for an hour of snowman making. At the end of my line the nymph hangs from the slightest tippet: almost unworldly in this world of absolute clarity. The river is as clear as . . . well . . . as ice. And I imagine to myself that this isn't water I'm fishing but some form of liquid ice, or the inside of a child's Christmas snow scene. I'm in the crystal ball and the snow is falling like feathers.

Perhaps because of the way the light slants this time of year, or perhaps because of the particular pensive slant of my imagination, I drift between the literal world of the river in front of me and the other world of the river I have in my head. On the winter river, as I see it today, everything looks clearer, somehow closer. I remind myself that what I'm walking is really the till of the glacier. An odd thought that I'm fishing in the belly wash of the last gasp of the ice age.

I remind myself, looking up toward the white ridge along the river, that the rocks at my feet

slipped slowly out of the glacier and may not have
moved far over the last ten thousand years. I slow
my pace, lift a few pebbles from the bottom, knowing that sometime in the dead cold of February I'll
take them out, lay them on the desk and sort and re-
sort, put them in my mouth and taste: glacier, a hint
of iron.

With the stones absorbing body heat in my pocket, I cast a summer cast, or a late fall cast, thinking
again of the time I floated through here in a river-
boat with the lightning dancing overhead, and suddenly I remember to slow down. December fishing
rhythm is slower, steadier, more measured . . . a way
of keeping yourself warm as well as a method of
delivering a fly. Fishing the winter river seems more
meditative. With no intrusion from the human
world, the mind has a way of opening up, even
though the cold is knocking at the door of the
warmest parts of your interior. So, meditative and
cold, as if I were in some Japanese print, I move
slowly, like the ice moves downriver.

The water I'm moving through is as haunted as
any I know. For over twenty years I've left parts of
myself here, first as a resident and now as a visitor.
In fact, just downstream there's a stump I call the
"quarter hole": once in a moment of absolute bore-
dom when a Hendrickson hatch didn't happen I
slipped a quarter into the deeply decayed fracture of

an old cedar. Now, I do it every time I pass through, the quarters giving off a soft glint, a silver matte patina etched by the daily abuse of the weather.

Back in the real world, the snow makes the river clearer in my head, the water mirroring a grey sky. I think of the river, the sky, the other interior river I carry inside me and tend carefully in my imagination: a dream river where all loss and despair disappear. A dream river where all the rivers of my life merge into one, while back on this river everything seems to have gone into this perfect greyness, and I become lost in the grey of the river. If I could, I would trade my life, right here, right now, for a life on the river, let myself dissolve into the snow I see up ahead as the river literally vanishes downstream. "Where'd he go?" someone might ask at the bar. "Just disappeared once." Into the cold. Into the grey. Into the dream river.

So I move slowly downstream, half imagining, half dreaming the nymph at the bottom of pools, suspended like something frozen in ice. I think of its tiny humped body washing in currents I can't see, the wing case only slightly bulging, if at all. And then I think of the magnitude of fishing: this river, all this water and a single dark nymph swimming across the pool in front of me. And I think of the fish: just beginning to settle in to a winter of slower metabolism. Their tiny brains hazing over with the onset of months and months of snow, wind. Sleet. The constant freeze and the occasional thaw, the sun mostly a thin, ghostly disc in the sky. It's the fish I think of late at night all winter, how they hover, barely moving for hours, pacing themselves, their bodies rippling against the slow crush of icy water.

Right now, getting colder, I mull over my casting options as I stand above a pool, where in July, I catch fish on the surface. Instead, I know they're deep. Sulking, turning slowly every so often to take in a winter nymph. If you were down there with them, watching their eyes, their fins, you'd know that they move ever so slowly, economizing, hunkered down in the dark December water, almost oblivious to any form of casting. The list of procedures is short: a cast back upstream for a dead-drift, the Crosfield Pull or the Leisenring-Lift technique, none of which I'm even remotely familiar with on the loose from the study and the books, adrift here in the grey dream. I opt for a fourth move: the swimming nymph swing, though I doubt anything, fish or nymph, is capable of swimming in this weather.

I cast and drift, cast and drift, letting the dark nymph swim ever so slowly, wading past places I knew. Places I know now are more important to me than my own backyard. Just below Pine Road I head into the stretch of water where I used to spend almost every summer night. I smell the odor of the winter river now. The fresh scent of snow. The odor of cedar and iron. Swamp gas. And I smell, as I did three springs ago, the acrid smell of fire. Up the bank I can still see the blackened trunks of trees, the swaths left by the rage of forest fire. For an instant, wading between the charred banks, I think I see the ghost dogs of friends, killed by smoke and flames, rise up out of the snow, their bodies whole, black again. I want them to leap into the river, but they drift over me and land on the other charred shore, vanishing into the woods.

I stopped fishing. Tried to start again, worked and fought with the idea of the dogs coming back to life in my head and then felt my heart sink, cold and heavy. I gave in and then headed for the truck. Walking back along the high bank past the water I had just fished, I realize that I had come up empty. No strikes. No fish. Nothing but chapped hands, throbbing knees, the cold deep inside me now. Somehow, that was the way it was supposed to be: destined when I left Interlochen, the leather book of weighted nymphs in the warmth of a fishing vest, my head awash with the smell of my wife's skin, the warm touch of a daughter's goodbye kiss, and the humid, wondrous odor of my golden retriever. The warmth of home.

I reminded myself of the great joy of fishing, even in the cold, even when your hands froze around the

butt of a rod and you had to suck on the line guides
to free them up, the small dots of ice drifting in your
mouth, almost like small nymphs of pure ice.
Suddenly, I was struck by opposing forces of desire: I
wanted to go home and I wanted to stay on the river.

I wanted the ghosts of the fire dogs to come back,
their coats black and glistening in the healing water
of the river. I wanted them to slide up to me in the
current, whole again. I wanted the jackpine to suddenly turn green and I wanted to look downriver
once more and see the iris beds in full bloom, the
damselflies moving like small, dark clouds.

I wanted to hole up and build a small fire, warm
my hands and face enough to want to get back into
the water. In the last light of a perfect December
afternoon I wanted to slip back into the river, fish just
one more bend. I wanted to feel the slight touch of a
delicate trout mouth, its jaws turning a nymph over
and over. And then I wanted to disappear, live like a
dog along the river so that I could come home and
say that I had given myself over to water, to the ele-
ments, that I had rolled the stones and come up wild
and above all, that I had wintered over.

Walking the River, December

I walk upstream on one of those mornings when, if you look behind you, the rising sun is casting gold light into the trees. All the leaves are down and there is snow coming in from the west, the sky an inky black. At thirty degrees, without the five layers that protect me, I wouldn't last more than a few minutes before my body shut down. Upriver, in a shallow gravel run there are old river browns in the last sideways dances of their fall spawning. The river here is clear and cold. In the water, if you watch closely enough, you can see the slightest motions of their gills, how their mouths move up and down almost imperceptibly, their fins holding them in a perfect balance between water and sky.

Bring a trout out of the water and into the air and he suffocates. But underwater, in the cold, liquid atmosphere of a stream, his body, moves the way the current moves. His skin ripples and gives against the current. Imagine an automobile with a flexible skin heading into the wind. How it might move and shift according to pressure. Add the tiny platelets of thousands of scales and you'd have skin that was able to

take the shape of the air itself. A trout, bound only
by the limits of its skeleton, the literal stretch of its
skin, is close to being made of river itself.

Reading and research tell us "that the blood and
body fluids of trout have salinity of about 0.6 per-
cent, higher than that of fresh water." Translated into
the language of the fisherman, that means that on
freshwater rivers, water is constantly "diffusing into
their bodies" through the delicate tissues of their
mouths and gills. The fish keep an internal balance
by "excreting large amounts of very dilute fluid" back
into the river. Think of a trout as membranous, the
barriers between river and muscle as microscopic
and you'll know that trout are literally a form of the
rivers they live in.

Just before you release a fish from your hand, let
your fingers slip down its sides while you hold it in
the water. In that meeting of the two worlds, you
above the water line, the trout below, you are finally
able to understand that the slightest pressure from
the water means the slightest yield of its skin.

Back in the shallows the fish surge and slip sideways into each other. Egg and milt meet, settle
toward the safe harbor of the gravel below. All winter
the trout grow into the river, the water moving over
them, past them, through them.

I dip my hand into the water, holding it against
the current. In less than a minute it goes numb. I

leave it there as long as I can stand. Minutes later
I'm dancing in front of the fireplace, my hand close
to the flames, my skin coming back to life, the air of
the room dense with the iron smell of the river running just below the window.

Middle Distance:
The Balm of Water

I am reminded daily, as I look toward an imaginary spot a mile and a half out in Green Lake, that there is great value in staring into the middle distance. There's nothing out there, of course, except sixty feet of clear water. Sky. I've been over that spot hundreds of times in the boat and looked back toward the house, but the effect isn't the same.

Essentially, the middle distance is that one spot where you hope to find some sense in your life. I stare into that space hoping to find some semblance of sanity or what it must mean to take the fabric of my life, hold it up in front of me and see a recognizable pattern. Or else, I hope to watch the clouds form and re-form, see my past, present and future played out up there. In essence, I want a clue. I simply want to know that after the subtraction of effort, pain, anxiety, fear and longing what I'll end up with is the clear-eyed notion that what's left is valuable.

Though my life has been relatively free of trauma, I seek the solitude of water to replenish my faltering soul engines left depleted by the workaday world. If I'm lucky, the healing comes in waves, an inundation.

There are days, sometimes, weeks in the summer when I am able to give myself the luxury of either staring at the middle distance of Green Lake or fly-fishing on the AuSable. The effect is the same: a release from the chaos that spins around each of us in the form of popular culture, noise, debt, greed and avarice.

I suppose, when I look back at what few things I've managed to write in the last twenty years, that the single binding influence in what creative power I have is the balm of moving water. As Gary Snyder says, "Creativity is not at its best when it's a by-product of turbulence." The great engine of anxiety which used to drive my poems started failing years ago. In fact, I'd chuck it all and trade every poem I ever wrote for a piece of tangled, lost river frontage and the simple pleasure of measuring time in terms of spring runoff, insect hatches, moon phases and hydrological tables.

Lately each day I've found myself seated at the window more often, my vision blurred by early November storms. In that middle distance I see myself dancing in some kind of cloud/mist vision and I am reminded of a passage from "Night Highway Ninety-Nine" by Gary Snyder:

"Sokei-an met an old man on the banks of the
Columbia River growing potatoes & living all
    alone,
Sokei-an asked him the reason why he lived there,
he said,
Boy, no one ever asked me the reason why.
I like to be alone.
I am an old man.
I have forgotten how to speak human words."

That's the beauty of hovering out there in that
middle distance: no words to speak, no need for language. Out there the world falls away. But here, hunkered down in the house, I sense myself getting older. I know I have one day left for every two I've lived. Each morning after going into this water-fueled meditation I rise to the tasks at hand, healed enough to withstand the wounds of each day. At the window, staring out, I give myself over to a dream of someday living quietly, sustained by the notion that I will take up residence in the middle distance, forgetting once and for all how to speak human words.

Winter: Dancing at the Edge of Nothing

From up here, in my house, twenty feet above Green Lake I can look out across three miles of ice and lose track of the following things:

Time
Sense
Speaking
Self

This is my hill here on the world every winter. I've abandoned almost all my fantasy pursuits, giving my life over, as Tom McGuane says, to a "diminishing portfolio of enthusiasms." The poems stacked in the basement and arranged in a few "slim volumes" as the critics say, are barely a hedge against mortality much less this bitter cold. I suppose I could take a few hundred pages, rip them out and cover the windows. Hunker down. But I'd miss what I'm looking at right now.

My fly rods are idle in the corner next to the window. Outside, the wind and sun make the lake seem more like a great salt flat. I imagine the men in shanties not as the perpetually unemployed, the bored, the marriage-wrecked, the early morning beer drinkers they probably are, but as priests of silence. Their shanties, some of them looking like the back ends of house trailers, seem more like outposts, hermitages. More than once I've been out on the lake at night, wandering past frozen holes covered with whole pine trees, and stood near the doors of these shelters. Inside I can hear voices, muttering, and see the thin light slipping out around the ice. On these nights I think of men hunched over their fishing holes, their own eyes glazing over, bending closer, looking into that other world as if they were looking into God's eye itself.

Later, when I'm back home I fall asleep dreaming that the inside of my head is like one of those ice-bound asylums. I look down into the half-lit abyss of myself and I see the abyss staring back. Nietzsche was right. Sometimes, in the dream, I'm holding a spear, terrified that what's below me will not kill easily. Other times, I dream I'm the fish and that there is a world of madmen above me.

During the day I hear anchor ice chocking up against bone marrow, and feel the lake inside every part of me that is still alive, every part not blasted out by cold and numbness and the constant lack of sun. So I follow the same pattern for weeks: staring for hours into the vast white of the lake and then dreaming the lake all over again at night.

There are no maidens in these waters. No anima figures surfacing in the spearing hole between my boots. No kisses offered up to warm even a cubic inch of a frozen heart. This is deadly territory. This is the winter place where your soul either sleeps and dies or rises, almost in individual particles on the first surge of spring.

I know, in the midst of a mayfly hatch this summer, I'll make the move just as I've done thousands of times: flicking my wrist, the fly line arcing toward nymphing rainbows. The old ice of February will rattle down from my skull and lodge itself forever in my wrist. If I could, I'd walk out of here, burn my winter clothes at the end of the driveway, ditch the snow shovel under the wheels of the first snowplow I see, then hitch to someplace in the jungle where ice is still a mystery.

Following the Pull in the Blood

Almost all of my adult life has been given over to a love of rivers. When I sift through what I've done and what I do, the most prominent element of my life always comes back to the moving water of streams, creeks and rivers. Other people may own a portion of my time and my attention bought and paid for, but no one owns my imagination. So it is that most of my waking hours are spent in the ever specific waking dreams of fly-fishing on a stretch of water on the AuSable that I have fished so often, I could fish blind.

I count the days on the calendar marking several wondrous events: birthdays, Christmas and the Opening Day of trout season. I give religious significance to Opening Day, not for the fishing, which is usually marginal, but for the pure joy of being with beloved friends sitting by the edge of a river. The sacrament is Spanish coffee, laced with volatile liqueurs.

For almost the last twenty years I've spent Opening Day with the same people. They know the river and like me, carry it under their skin throughout the year. We always sit on the porch, despite inclement weather, and sip our coffee watching the river move like a vein below us.

Deep in the belly of a dark winter I find myself sifting through photographs of us on the porch. Almost everything I want from my life rides in those photos. I love my lovely wife and daughter and I love the major part of my life I know is anchored to them, something in me settled, peaceful. But even before Opening Day I'll feel that old pull in the blood, something still wild, then pack up the car and take them with me.

We'll travel east and walk into the cabin by midmorning. Outside the river will be slipping past, high and full. I'll take the cup of Spanish and drink it slowly and feel my life rubbing against all that I love. During those languid hours of Opening Day I'll sort and re-sort my priorities, shuffling them like a deck of Tarot cards knowing everything will come up with something about rivers.

There on the porch, I'll whisper the secret I speak every day: I want my life in rivers. I want the healing power of water to linger in all my wounds. I want to one day look in the mirror and see a face that looks like an Edward S. Curtis photograph: the skin etched and burnished by river weather, a face like a map, each line and wrinkle a tributary, knowing I traded whatever I could find for the balm of moving water.

Dawn Streamers

Five A.M. and there is almost no light. What I see is ambient, glancing, not streaks but a faint greyness to the air. On the river everything blends together into grey mist. I hear the sound of water and smell the unmistakable odor of cedar, a heightened scent, thick and sweet in my nose. I stand like this for several minutes feeling the way I slide into this weather, how my body sluices through air and water just before I give myself over.

By 5:30 the sky has lightened. The fog rises off the surface of the water, the river revealing itself mostly in grey forms, rocks, hundreds of cedar sweepers, and pockets of dark, still water. I bypass the boxes of dry flies, switch on my light and open my streamer book. They're all there, attractors, deceivers, the combinations. Like a book, I read the flies and imagine each one underwater, how the current brings marabou alive, turns colors more vivid, how the movement of water helps to bring the fish to the hook.

I choose a Queen Bess, a local pattern, a size 8 on a long shank hook, tie it on and stare upriver into

the greyness. A decade of fishing this same water
and the pockets back up under the cedars where
marauding browns strike before daylight is set in the
deep bed of my memory.

I cast and arc my fly under overhanging branches,
twitching the streamer through pocket water watching for the instant surges, the boiling of fish. I fish
like this until the sky opens to half blue, feeling the
slam of strikes, several fish put against the reel.

I cast and retrieve, cast and retrieve, watching the
streamer settle, moving downriver trying to lose
myself in the rising fog, the swirl of mist. 6:15 and
the sun cracks the tree line and all the warmer air
from the river rushes upward, and for several minutes I think of myself as truly lost. If someone found
me years later they'd notice the grey of the river in
my skin, the dark flecks of gravel in my hair, the
smell of swamp in every pore.

On the way back to the cabin I sit on a high bank
and look down through the early April light, hoping
to see a glimpse of myself still down there, dissolving
into the river. Each cast comes back, sewing itself
into a net of memory, the weight of each fish still
vibrating in my arm.

King of the Brook Trout

Smoke and mirrors: the vision of a career that is not a vision but a kind of mental sinkhole. All I ever wanted was to be king of the brook trout. Maybe king in just one county or on one river or even a stretch of one river. A hundred yards of one river. With a small cabin and a fireplace. A shirt made of brook trout skins. Nothing to do but fish and cut wood for heat. Smelling of pine smoke and fish. A shack, mostly in the mind, but a shack for keeping myself away from the world.

Things started to go downhill, or uphill, depending on where you're looking from, when I stopped talking. You can't stop talking and be a teacher at the same time. I had, for twenty-three years, talked, mostly. I hadn't really taught anything, really. Just talked. Babbling, I called it late in the career I had as a teacher. I taught literature and writing mostly to students who didn't seem to care much. And for the most part I cared way more than they did.

My great trick as a teacher wasn't that I convinced hundreds of students that I knew something, but that I could daydream. When I was talking about Hemingway, or Fitzgerald, or Stephen Crane, I was really fly-fishing on the AuSable. One day, in mid-sentence about Nick Adams, I looked into their faces and instead saw the river. They vanished. I spoke what to them must have been a foreign language. I spoke of hatches and flies, sections of river, how to dead drift a nymph, how to cast and retrieve early in the morning up under the cedar sweepers. I moved my arms in casting motions and flailed the air in the room. When I finished, the room was empty. The principal stood outside, his glasses pressed up against the small glass of the door. When I went past him I could hear his high-pitched voice, words came and went, "Contract," "Obligations," "You're on tenure" . . . and I left.

That was years ago, it seems, only it was just a month or two. What have I been doing? I've made deep visits to the interior. My own. I found a place along the river, well past the edge of town I knew some day I'd find, that spot where the road drops into the ravine, peters into a two-track and finally nothing. The guard hairs rose on my neck and I danced for an hour under the dark sky, then carried all my poems from the trunk to a place so utterly worthless no one else would bother to stop. I dropped the poems haphazardly, the reams of each year's work falling onto a reckless bonfire. I invoked

the remaining gods: the god who had rested on my
back and ridden me hard all my life, the god of lust
who hunched in my groin, the god of whiskey and
the god of longing drunk again on this last night, the
god of a lifetime of nightmares and the animal gods,
road kill gods, bird of prey gods, rabid-dog gods, and
the huge snake gods coiled just outside the firelight.
And when it was over, when all the gods had
acknowledged my last prayers of absolution, the fire
dying down, I reached for an ember, begged the
weeping god of my body to leave me here spread
over the coals, catching fire, rising for good on a
tongue of smoke.

So I abandoned my teaching life. My writing life
disappeared. I took up the fishing life. I fished for
days, then months, In all kinds of weather. I fished
mostly for brook trout. Each time I took one for food,
I saved its sacred skin and made it a part of a brook
trout skin shirt. Now, when I come in from the river
and hang it near the fire, I can still see tiny patches of
color, the way the light glints off the softened scales.

I am in my fishing place. My cabin made from the
debris left for worthless: old boards, river logs, pieces
of cloth here and there. A fire barrel floated down at
the end of the first hard month of rain I spent under
a tarp.

I live the river life and I know this river better
than anyone should. I look at my hands and see the

bends, the sweepers, the best and deepest pools, the slicks where feeding rainbows suddenly appear every June at the same time. When I fall asleep I smell the river in my skin and when I look in the mirror I see the river in my face.

You can't find this place. There are no roads in. No trails. I'll tell you this, though. Like I said, I know this river better than anyone should. When I came, I had visions of being some kind of a king of the brook trout. Then I realized that I wanted to only be the brook trout king of this river. And now, all I want is to claim the few bends above and below the cabin. I'd cut my own heart out to say that and have it be true.

Whether or not I'm fishing, I'm always in the river: Always my heart drifts out of me and each trip away from the water I feel a part of myself settle toward bottom. When I first came here I remembered a line from a poem I'd written: "Where do I find the dark lips of the river to offer the ragged edges of my life for healing." Everyday I offer myself up and everyday I come back healed.

PART 11

INTO THE BLACK RIVER

　　　　　To step
back from this swinging man twisting clockwise
is to see how we mine ourselves too deeply,
that way down there we can break through the soul's
rock into a black underground river that sweeps us
away.

　　　　—Jim Harrison, "Returning to Yesenin"

River Ghazals

1

All night I cruise bottom, my life an ice dream,
closed river mouths.

At the river she slipped down out of the air:
a woman with skin to be written on.

Not beside the river, but in the river,
rolling again and again toward deadfall.

The river's true heart: a cold spring under my flesh,
eyes blue as ice.

On the night river I trade my life for the lips of darkness.

2

Trade work for sleep. Trade sleep for hunger.
Give the hunger back to yourself.

The dog buried under the trees rises nightly,
carries a dream in her mouth.

A day of high clouds, the odor of honeysuckle
absorbed through her skin.

Dream dog, lick my wounds, take this body with you,
both of us drifting the river.

At the edge of the river a soul drops its kindling,
builds a small fire.

3

Three women slip out of the shadow of my life,
their lips brushing me like feathers.

A soul extinguishes itself, drifts toward the dark
    bottom where all loss comes to rest.

Always her voice: a river stone with a song inside,
or dying from the bones outward.

Suddenly, a man turns luminous, walks out of his life,
    gives himself to water.

4

There was a year of snow, dogs attacking the house,
silence frozen into muscle.

On the maps the weather raged.
Down below, I read the book of her skin.

An all day rain, the kind of rain that turns you shiftless
watching the empty road.

Let me love the humidity of her body,
the dark storm of her hair.

Watching the rain hit the river, eating brook trout,
rain in the fire, a life speaks back from the coals.

5

Think of your life as wind through a doorway.

Whenever you can, trade the bank for the river,
the sky for the bird, your skin for pure light.

Fuel your heart with single caresses, glances,
the sudden visions of your life gone feral.

Go to anyplace where there are more rivers than roads;
trade your flesh for any moving water.

Think of your life as a trigger, death in the target,
something blazing inside your chest.

6

Here, near the river, a day was lost, then another.
The heart turned inward, collapsing to a blister of pitch.

Yesterday the river was burnished by light, like brass.
I wanted to lie down, stretch molten sixty miles to the
    lake.

I walk the charred banks, the ghost dogs of friends com-
    ing up out of the ground. I try to weep them back to
        life in the river.

Each day I carry my body to the river, counting the
    bones.
Each day I count less, my body sifting away.

Pray to the water gods: no seams in your life.
A hand enters the river, disappears. A life in the current.

7

One last cast: a beautiful woman rises from the pool
    of sorrow
in my stomach. The full moon, clouds ripped apart in the
    wind.

Hold the darkest part of yourself over the water. Pray for
    sleep, a white water dream, the belly of the river
        against yours.

Just now, a brook trout slipping out of the mouth of a
    god.
The way light cuts through water, nations of stones.

I sat at the head of a sandbar covered with stones.
I stared, counted. Put it back together in a dream.

The body buried under the river: a mouth at last full of
    silence. A spirit rising like fog, the breath of the
        swamp.

8

Matthiessen alive on the River Styx. A great bird lifting off
    from under a shroud.

I gave my life away. Sent the skin to each compass point,
prayed that something still alive would drift back home.

All up and down the river: birds coming in to feed.
Inside my chest, my heart thinks it has wings, tries to fly.

What sound other than water can keep you alive?
Know the voice you choose to speak your name.

9

A river tattoo: on each arm another place to wish to die
for. In the mirror I see my eyes rising like two moons
over dark country.

In her sleep a daughter builds a raft. The perfect fit of her
body against the single oar as she drifts away.

Upstream rain, the river filling.
I walk home with the river aching in my legs.

I gave an eye to the river. Once a month the moon gives it
back, then weeks of blindness, her body smelling like
wet stones.

Her spine outlined against the last light on the river: a
place between her breasts where water pools, cools
the fever.

10

FOR JIM

23 years ago I read the ghazals for the first time,
and there near the river, something flew out of my skin.

Tonight, a full moon. I'm miles from where I need to be.
   All this living, then: moonlight down the hill moving
      like a river.

Carry your heart to the river. Pull the wings out from
   under your coat. Use your life like a talon, beak,
      tearing loose.

Get back: to swamps, to feeder creeks that have no
   names, those places where your life turns and follows
      the current.

One river ends, falls out of the body. The shadow of a
   man turns upstream, never looks back.

11

The Theory and Practice of Rivers: each day goes by, the
current boiling around the rock you have made of
your life.

Asleep by the river a dream rises up off the bottom. Your
chest cleaves, something with a heart made of water
slides in.

Woman to be river, river to be flesh, night to last. You
pray for a lifetime to be washed up against her.

In the knot of deadfall I saw how a life tangles, then how
part of the body drifts off, collects downstream to heal
itself.

Follow the tracks to their disappearing. Find the origin of
all rivers where time is cutting herself into ever smaller pieces.

12

This morning: a dream of all the rivers I've found in dreams.
All day: The great pleasure of water lodged under the flesh.

He went crazy. Built a cabin far from friends, saved himself
    for countless trips into the interior. Made fires, read the
        coals.

Where the river flows into another river: your blood moving
    at the speed of light, body a miracle of confluences.

Take this down: one dream a week you must wake inside
    the heart of the river. Come back to tell it.

The story goes like this: he conjured himself into a river.
Lay prone for days, his eyes following a sea of stars.

13

FOR DAVE

I shape my life to the weather. Twelve degrees and falling.
　　Each cast curling into the wind, driving snow, the sun
　　　　a dream.

How many times do I say the dead man's name to pull
　　him back? How many times do I dip my hand into the
　　　　river expecting a miracle?

I would bring him up into the light. Give him his old
　　name back.
Build a fire, tell him to stay close, back to the wind.

On the Betsie I lift the bodies of salmon from the river,
　　take them to the sand bar, read the maps of their skin.

In my own fire near the river mouth I see his eyes. My
　　body tries to drift off, learn the topography of the river
　　　　bottom.

Today, I wanted to forget my name, leave my life packed
　　in this skin near the river, pass away from this place.
　　　　Pass away.

PART III

THE DREAM RIVERS

Thinking how good it is to come up the path from the river, chimney smoke sifting above the trees, to open the cabin door and find myself still there, stirring logs in the stove

—Judith Minty, *Yellow Dog Journal*

The River Inside

1

Weeks go by, then months, the river iced over.
There's no particular place to walk, and each trail to
the river is covered again by the time I walk back to
the house. Each night before I go to bed I walk to the
edge of where I think the bank and the river come
together. I lie down with my ear pressed against the ice,
listening: This deep vein of water rises north of me,
comes down through cedar swamps and meadows, the
clear gravel riffles near Grayling. I think to myself on
this ten below night that there isn't a voice down there,
only an echo. I'm tempted to tell myself I hear things in
the current, or sense, in the slow rising of bubbles
trapped against ice, that I recognize the message. But
there is no message. No voice here in the night coming
from the belly of the river. This is the kind of night
when anchor ice is born, when the river stiffens. Weeks
from now, when the spring rains come, what's left will
sweep the river clean, the ice cutting through deadfall,
moving rocks for miles downriver. In August, if you're
lucky, you can bend down into a pool and find a piece
of river shale marked and cut, a kind of sign language

left as a reminder that there is no time, no day or week, no month, no full moon, no new moon. Only the slow, constant motion of water and ice, the heave of seasons, the river's long life only getting longer.

2

Back low in the trees the full moon is gathering
itself to lift over my head. Upstream the river has the
broken castings of moonpath, the dimples of hundreds
of tiny fish rising. In the swamp my body turns away
from the world, away from roads. I sit under the
sweepers of a hundred-year-old cedar, and watch night
sift in from the marsh. A nighthawk sluices downriver,
the deep "vrooo" of its voice a perfect language for the
way the sky and the river switch places. When I stand
to speak into the woods I say only my name. I say who
I am into the dark and nothing comes back. I wait
after each telling and then turn my name into a ques-
tion. What I hear is only current, the way water
deflects from deadfall, a way silence has of catching in
the throat. What good comes of this repeated calling,
this sending out of my name? This silence? Hours later
when I slide into bed, I think I hear something like I
have never heard coming from my lips: a voice like
darkness itself, the words rising from my belly, filling
the room with something dark and empty as if I were
calling back through forty years, my lips alive with
whatever it was I had lost.

3

For days now I have come to the river without fishing on my mind, seeking only the way the current takes
things away. I drop bits of leaves, pine needles into the
river and watch them head downstream. I put my hand
in and watch it vanish, then my arm and shoulders and
suddenly I am sliding my torso toward bottom, only my
head holding in the wash of the Platte. Underwater, my
eyes dissolve away, the sun only a memory, the smell of
river intensified in whatever it is that I have let myself
become. Somewhere downstream under a logjam,
under roots, in a bed of gravel, my body comes back to
itself, rising up through cool morning air. I carry this
sense home: water sifting through rock, through skin,
through bone, through memory. Water taking the mind
away from itself as if the hands of water could sort and
cleanse, and then turn the self loose back into the
world. Tonight, walking the hills near the house, I lift
my hands to my face and taste the river on my fingers,
some small part of me miles away, sidling back and
forth in the current, darkness just now settling over the
river.

4

Under the bridge I watch the salmon roll and spawn.
Later, downstream, I take a drink of death water, my lips
falling away. All up and down the river, birds coming in
to feed. Inside my chest, my heart thinks it has wings,
tries to fly. I speak my own name into the shifting light
of an October afternoon, send it out over the water. I
speak the names of fish, the birds, all the plants I know. I
try to lift off from this place, but my feet won't leave the
edge of the river. I squat down near a sandbar and try to
memorize the way the rocks have been nudged into
place, each stone a marker, a leaving, some way the river
has of keeping track of its past. Two old salmon sweep
by, their bodies dark and mottled. They move upstream,
death riding on their backs. A female rolls toward the
male next to her. On the surface of the river I see the
reflections of bright maples, and there, in that other
world underwater, I watch them spawn then drift back
downriver. I think of how the afternoon gathers itself,
how it is that a man can come to the edge of a river and
watch death swim by, then go home to make love, or
merely look out the window long enough to see himself
struggling to get the rider away from his life. And in his
sleep he knows the river is moving, the salmon are
rolling. Creatures are being ridden to exhaustion.

5

All night I have wandered the woods, headed deeper
into the Deadstream. At the river's edge I trace the
path of the moon as far upriver as I can see. Mayflies
drop out of the air, the surface of the river dimpled
with thousands of dying flies. I cast upstream, follow
the drift, mending line, always mending. In the semi-
dark, in the moonlight, I think I see the outline of my
own body as it steps from under the darker arms of
cedar sweepers. I stand perfectly still and when it passes directly in front of me, I hear it whisper: "Think of
what is left of your life as the water that is passing in
front of you right now." I step back on the bank and
watch myself trail downriver, then take off my clothes
and swim upstream, my mouth gathering in as much
water as possible, moonlight, the wash of river.
Wounds I thought I had forgotten suddenly heal,
something inside my life gathers itself, turns further
inward, lets the river pass through.

6

Today, high clouds being torn apart in the wind.
Each time I come home from the river I feel the precip-
itate of walking upstream, sitting at the smallest of
waterfalls where a feeder creek feeds into the Platte. I
leave stones there every time, tiny markers, one or two
placed in the wash of cold spring water. This afternoon, walking up the drive to get the mail I took a
river stone from my pocket, thought of how it was
formed by heat and pressure in a time almost before
time. Back inside, I put the stone back in the tiny river
I have made on top of my desk, each stone perfect,
each one a reminder of the message of what was left
behind. Tonight, just before I fall asleep, I'll watch this
little river like I watch the real one, sure there are fish
in every pool, something alive in the trees and deadfall.
And when sleep comes I'll carry stones back to the
dream river, put them back where they belong.

7

When I wake up in the middle of the night I listen for the river, the hiss of rain again, the memory there in the dark of another language I thought I had forgotten. In almost pitch black I hunch down by what's left of the fire, stir the hot ash with a piece of pine kindling. What catches fire comes like a word out of the ground, sifting up through the trees moving slowly away from this place where I have come to forget what I know, forget my own face, my skin, the way I speak. I taste the ashes, carry the voice of embers back to the tent. Before I fall back to sleep I taste the burnt pitch on my tongue. I think of new words for trees, the sky, the way my life has hung in some odd kind of balance all these years. And I think of how the river moves past this camp in the dark, this place where a man is just now struggling to speak something he does not know.

The Dream Rivers

1

Lost again, this time on the Pere Marquette and up ahead the snow forms into the torso of someone you never had the chance to know. This is the place they'll find you in the spring: two legs dancing in the current, your neck tied with twenty-pound monofilament, one eye slightly askew, the grin on your face from a week of ecstasy, the way you imagined her torso to drape down over you like a shroud, how she moved with the motion of the river, and because she was made of snow, how her skin settled into your own.

2

You wash up in your sleep, your belly white, eyes opaque, like tiny moons floating in your skull. You love this ritual, this way all of the women in your life come to you with intentions of rescue, how they slip their hands under your head, letting the river pass over you. One of them whispers that all the rivers on earth were once rivers of blood and to live once meant finding that one true river, cutting yourself open, wading in, letting the river pass through, the women sifting into your eyes, your hair, your body like a river.

3

I see them sometimes, walking the banks when I
fish, their arms raised in a half wave, their faces con-
torted. Even from the middle of the river I know on
each face I see a little of my own, knowing that these
ghosts are only husks, collections of bad dreams, lost
places, remembrances of all the things I never was.
Some are the spirits of relatives dead thirty years too
soon, the ghosts of alcoholics, horse thieves, prisoners
of war. For hours I have fished and seen them drift off
bottom, their huge eyes blue and clear, then my life
feels as if it separates. Half of me goes downstream
fishing between deadfallen cedar, the other half slips
in, lies down in familiar arms, goes back wild to the
river.

4

One river falls out of the moon, the other begins in
a photograph from the 20s; Hemingway up in
Michigan, stepping off a boxcar, the flare strapped like
an antennae to his pack, headed north, tramping the
streams, each twist of his wrist, each cast arcing
toward that last day in Idaho when the shotgun lay in
his hands, the barrel icy, a thousand rivers releasing all
at once.

5

Once, on the Platte, the moon, stars, reflected in a
cup of whiskey, the mirror image of one eye looking
through itself, like peering in the front of a pin hole
camera. Only you look back, see your father casting
before you were born. The line moves away from him
like light, and you feel that pull, how he baptized you
with a handful of river water when you were eight
years old, gave the first drink and then drank himself,
and each movement now is a memory of how the river
moved that night, how your father has river in him,
how your river is the same as your father's.

6

Maps turn red, rivers turn to blood. A body stands,
is part map: the ghosts of rivers haunt the veins, casting under half moons, knowing there are fish struggling out of the heart.

7

"Water will never leave earth" you wrote, and
tonight I send what little is left of my spirit toward
that black feeder creek near the house, then sit down
back inside and watch, waiting for its return, thinking
how my spirit will look when it comes in the back door,
holding a woman made entirely of water, thinking how
my spirit would enter this woman, run the darker
regions inside her, ride the current of her wildness
home.

The River Everywhere

FOR CLAUDIA

1

Under the sky, under the bed, under the house, the most beautiful woman I have ever seen is stepping out of her skin, as if out of delicate silk. She holds her skin in her hands as if it were cloth and begins to wring it slowly, and slowly, the most beautiful water begins flowing. When she lifts this water up into this world, her hands cup toward my face and when I drink her, I know for the first time that her river is where I have lived my whole life.

2

Even before I realized it, a river was following me underground. When I slept, it stopped moving and stayed like a shadow under the bed. And when I fished, it coursed, just above bedrock. Once, I remember hearing this river, like a voice from a closet, or a cellar, a place where the husk of a life fell into itself and was saved by the breath of the river.

3

The river is running now over the desk, through my hands, running in the white threads of my shirt, moving in each molecule of my hair. Upstairs I hear my wife and daughter laughing while the current sifts past their bodies. When I go up the stairs they are both resting like stones on the floor, the river running translucent over them, like a second skin.

4

When my daughter falls asleep I hear the river running under her bed, a dream river now and I hear her building a raft in her dream and want to stop her from pushing off. All night I hear her voice calling from downriver, trailing off. I slide toward her mother. Our love is water. I pray to whatever water god would trade the days I have left to turn our lives to water, so that in the instant our lives meet there will be no seam, no difference in the current of her body and the current of mine.

PART IV

INTO THE BACK COUNTRY

We were following a long river into the mountains.
"Finally we rounded a ridge and could see deeper in—
the farther peaks stony and barren, a few alpine trees.
Ko-san and I stood on a point by a cliff, over a rock-
walled canyon. Ko said, "Now we have come to where
we die."
I asked him, what's up there,
then-meaning the further mountains.
"That's the world after death." I thought it looked
just like the land we'd been travelling, and couldn't
see why we should have to die.
Ko grabbed me and pulled me over the cliff–
both of us falling. I hit and I was dead. I saw
my body for a while, then it was gone. Ko was there
too. We were at the bottom of the gorge.
We started drifting up the canyon. This is the way to
the back country."

—Gary Snyder, "Journeys"

Last Pool

I SUPPOSE, NOW THAT I'M TELLING THIS, no one will believe me. I'll admit to the far-fetched notion of it: finding a place where trout, big trout, would spend their last days. After all, how many of us have seen a trout die a natural death? Can you even think of the time when you looked down and saw a fish holding, his body perfect, only to roll suddenly away with the current, surfacing downstream, his white belly pointed toward the sky? On the skin of it, this story sounds like it's about elephants. Graveyards.

But I was there. Stood at the pool myself and watched the sun arc through a whole day while below me I watched the spotted backs of eight-pound browns shift in the slow sifting of current. I was, and am still, stupefied. Standing there, I measured my own senses. I thought I knew exactly where I had traversed the three bends of the river before it turned near the edge of the swamp. I was further sure, I kept telling myself that I was truly still on Simpson Creek. The Simpson Creek that passes through miles of cedar deadfall and hummocks, trickling past mucky banks only to move its three-foot width into the AuSable without even a ripple.

In my head I sensed my position as if I were standing in front of a topographical map and I had driven a pin into this place and said "here, I am exactly here." But I was wrong. I was on a creek, I think now, that has no name. I had wandered in well before daylight and gotten turned around somehow and found myself standing still in the swamp just listening.

At first light I moved north to where I thought Simpson Creek might be, but found myself, standing, miraculously on the edge of a pool perhaps ten feet across and no more than eight feet deep. The roots of huge cedars swept into it like fingers. More than a wide spot in a small stream, it looked like a spring of sorts. The bottom sand bubbled in places and fish moved in and out from under the bank. I counted thirty or forty fish, not sure they were all different, but sure they were large, larger, I knew, than any fish I had ever seen in the river.

I began to ask questions of myself: how . . . no, why had I found this place? For several minutes, which might have been an hour, I decided it was pure Providence, then I danced over to the side of luck and then back again.

I stayed with luck and good fortune as I put my rod together, then fingered over a ragged book of nymphs. I couldn't very well float a dry fly to deep cruising browns. In a clear pool. With no current on top. So I tied the most careful of knots on the smallest of tippets I could manage then stepped back from the pool to regain what little composure I had left.

I was trembling at this one single chance I had stumbled upon, or been given and I hesitated. Not wanting to spook the fish out of the pool, I knelt first and then crawled back, just as I had done as a child fishing brook trout on the brushy streams near Greenville with my father. Back then, we whispered and dropped our tiny hooks with leaf worms threaded onto them and we prayed. I actually heard my father praying over the bank of a small trout stream in Michigan. He prayed to his mother and to his father, and then he prayed to the god of fish.

So I lay there on the side of the pool trying to recall the fish prayer of my father. I thought about the water and the angle I wanted the nymph to follow as it drifted toward bottom. When I inched close enough to look, most of the fish had steadied, almost motionless an inch or two off the sandy bottom.

I watched for a while, wanting to know precisely where to set the nymph so it would look like a nymph falling, almost like a feather, through the clear water. In my mind I hooked, of course, the largest fish I could see and just as I began to reel him in I saw a fish suddenly roll up, as if it were taking a fly on the surface, only it went suddenly still. Then it turned belly up and floated to the surface of the pool, its gills moving almost imperceptibly.

I watched it circle the pool in the slow eddy of current and then it died completely. When it caught the full light of midday its colors had already started to fade. The other fish paid no attention. They moved up and down in the spring, banked slowly for tiny nymphs and then settled back down.

I stayed for an hour, maybe two. I watched the sun track through the trees. I moved back from the pool and drank an entire flask of whiskey. I looked repeatedly at my tackle. I ran my finger down the humped back of the nymph I'd wanted to use, imagined it so perfectly wet and deadly. Then I left.

I hadn't fished. It took hours to thrash my way out. I stood at the car and offered the prayer I had forgotten in my adrenaline haste. I looked at the sky. I looked at my hands. I put my rod away and drove home. In front of me the road turned slick in an early evening rain. In the rearview mirror the sky darkened and seemed ever closer. I tried to remember the way in, knowing the way memory has of closing up, turning the past into myth, tangling details into snarls of fact and fiction, then praised myself for not marking the way out.

The Coast of Nowhere

Thirteen miles inland from Lake Michigan I can still
hear the sound of the Platte River running over shallow
gravel, a voice so perfectly clear I hear it in every room
of the house, the pulse of river, the memory of current
loose in the walls. And tonight, walking the river mouth
near the house, I look up into the high branches of the
red pines and listen to the questions in the wind, the
way they sift through the delicate needles thirty feet in
the air and then seem to fall at my feet: one asks the way
into the heart, another asks whether the god of rivers
and lakes is sleeping inside my hands, and the third, the
one I cannot answer, asks if another decade of walking
this coastline will bring me answers.

Once in the house, I look down through almost a century of trees, then begin to take them inside slowly. I
pack the red pines closest to my heart, then lift in the
maples, the giant oaks, then the rocks scattered along
the shore. I take in the coastline, the river where it
enters the lake. Somewhere inside, this landscape comes
back together, each tree where it belongs, and the sky:
the way the sky looks from the deck, looking due south

toward the peninsula, staring hard into that middle distance two miles out in the middle of Green Lake, that spot where nothing seems to happen, only empty space, watching from the coast of nowhere, I tell myself, a spot where I send the worst of everything to straighten itself out.

Tonight, when I fall asleep, I'll dream walk this inner coast and when I pass my hands close to the trees I know, run them over rocks and stumps, they will glow like embers, this place so close to nowhere, so close.

What My Father Told Me

What my father told me, he mostly told me when
we were fishing. It didn't matter that we had skipped
church for the hundredth time, or whether he had
walked into my school and gotten me out of class. He
wanted to tell me things, he said, and the best place,
he felt, was on the river. He said the river was as close
to time as you were going to get. No sense, he said,
watching a clock to learn about time. It wouldn't even
do you any good to study rock stratification or fossils,
like some scientists believed.

What seemed to arrest my father's attention the
most was the fact that rivers were always full of water.
He would often stand on the banks of our cabin on the
North Branch and ask over and over where all that
water was coming from. Of course, he knew. And one
summer when it was over 90 for almost two weeks in a
row we sweated our way north of Lovells and found
the source: a small fingerlet seeping out from under a
hummock in a swamp. Another time we stopped along
the mainstream and my father showed me what he
called a sacred spot. There was an iron ring in the

ground, and looking into it was like peering into the eye of a river god, my father whispered.

My father taught me about perfection too. Often I heard him say "perfect, everything is perfect" and when I asked what he meant, he'd always say, "Just look around." But I remember him telling me a story about perfection, just to illustrate that perfection wasn't always an absolute quality in his life. Once in Montana he had been fishing a section of the Madison when he stopped in mid-cast to admire what he considered to be absolute perfection: a clear, evening sky, five-pound rainbows rising to midges, alone and miles from any house. Suddenly he heard the sound of tires squealing, then the crush of metal against the guardrail a hundred feet above him and a Ford Pinto flew over the exact spot where he was fishing, landed in the river and sank in front of him. The driver swam toward him, my father half cursing his bad luck, but marveling at his one chance to see a car fly.

He taught me about glaciers and about how glaciers literally carved out the bellies of rivers. Move this water out of here he'd say and all you got is a meandering single track through the woods barely deep enough to spit in, but add water and you've got a living vein. My father never talked much about God or religion except to say that whatever made rivers had to be wild.

My father loved wildness. He loved the fact that you could stand only so long in the current of a river until your feet started to drop out from under you. And he often said, over his shoulder when we were fishing together, that you could take something out of your imagination you didn't like, just like you would out of your pocket and let it go into the river and it would never come back.

He told me that whenever he felt any sense of failure, he would go to the river and just let whatever was bothering him loose in the water. He said he felt wild when he drank from the river, or caught brook trout and ate them on the same day. Trout particles he called them and he was sure they had lodged in his bloodstream over the years until, he said proudly, he was more brook trout than man.

When I was twelve he took me to the Upper Peninsula for a fishing trip on the Big Two-Hearted. He was careful to point out that the river wasn't the real river Hemingway was writing about, that was the Black, further east of the Two-Hearted. This was before the Mackinaw Bridge, when you had to take a ferry across the Straits. We holed up in the station wagon, listening to Ernie Harwell call a late Tigers game. I could smell the odor of wet canvas. Tents and fishing bags. Fishing tackle.

On our way into the river my father told me that of all the places he'd been, all the rivers he'd fished, this

place we were going meant the most. In the 40s he and
Fred Lewis had fished this water for weeks at a time.
Years later, when Fred went blind, his wife dropped
him off and he fished by himself for two weeks.

I still have pictures of Fred Lewis in my albums at
home. In one, he's wearing a red plaid wool shirt. My
dad says those were the best shirts you could wear to
fish in. He told me to always have a fishing shirt handy.
Never wear it for anything else, he said. And never,
never wash it. If you can, he said, the first time you
wear it, you need to anoint it with the blood of a few
night crawlers and brook trout.

That's what my father fished for most. Brook trout.
He could sneak into the smallest, brushiest streams
where you'd swear there wouldn't hardly be any water.
He'd dangle a short rod over the bank and slip the
worm in without making a ripple. Then he'd mutter a
prayer to the fish gods, to keep them close, he'd say, and
then he'd lift the tip of his rod so slowly you couldn't
see. I remember brook trout coming out of the clear
water, how they looked like miniature paintings vibrant
and loose with color.

My father told me sitting on the banks of the Two-
Hearted that the best way to cook brook trout was in
the coals. Pack them in river clay, he said and put it in
the fire. When the clay cracked, the fish was done.

We ate fish like that for a week. My father drinking
small glasses of wine. Sometimes he'd let me sip some

and we'd lean back against the trees, our faces hot from the flames. Coming through the fire, his voice sounded like the voice of a god. It sounded hollow and large, like it was coming from somewhere under the earth.

My father told me that rivers weren't really natural phenomena at all. Rivers, he said came directly out of the veins of the gods themselves. To prove it, he said, try to follow one. When you tromp through a swamp for a day or two, following something that's getting smaller and smaller and then finally vanishes under a hummock in some swamp somewhere, he said, you'd need to go down under the earth to find the source.

The source was in wildness, he said. A wild god making a river come up out of the ground by opening up one of his veins and letting his divine blood sift upward toward blue sky. When I think about my father now, I think about gods under the earth and about blood, about how he baptized himself there on the Two-Hearted that summer.

I'd already been baptized twice. Once in church when I was a baby, he said. But he'd had second thoughts about what went on, about who was sanctifying what. And another time by my grandfather with a handful of lake water. Now, he told me, I needed to drink from the same river that he drank from.

We were standing knee deep just about the mouth. Lake Superior was crashing below us. He lifted a cupped hand to my mouth and I drank and then he drank. Blood he whispered. Keep this wild blood in you for the rest of your life.

When my father wasn't working or fishing, his other great joy was quoting short lines of poetry while we fished. When he wasn't talking about the connection between rivers and the spiritual territory he tended so seriously inside me, he was talking about the wildness he loved in poets he'd read. I always thought it odd that a man brought up around huge tool and die presses would come to something so seemingly fragile as poetry. He particularly loved an ancient Irish poem, "The Wild Man Comes to the Monastery." Some nights when he was a bend or two below me I could hear him calling back, "though you like the fat and meat which are eaten in the drinking halls, I like better to eat a head of clean water-cress in a place without sorrow." At twelve, those lines meant little, but over the years, something seeped in and built up, an accumulation of images, he liked to say to me, would get me through the hard times when my life would go dark. To keep away the loneliness he'd say and then whisper another line from Machado, or Neruda. Keep these poets close to your heart, he would admonish me and so I fished for years listening to the great Spanish surrealists drifting upriver to me in the dark.

Weeks later we were drifting on Turk Lake trolling for pike. It was almost dark and my father was looking back over the transom, watching his line. One word came out of his mouth, storm. I looked into the western sky and saw huge clouds boiling in, black and inky, the curl of them like a huge wave. Keep fishing he said. Keep casting from the bow. The pike will feed just before it hits, keep casting, cast your heart out he said.

From where I stood I could see a white belly slashing up toward my lure. I could see my father etched by lightning, his rod low, then him striking, both of us fighting fish under the darkening sky.

We lost both fish. The sky seemed to literally fall on us. My father told me later in the cabin, that we'd been lucky, foolish, but lucky he said. He told me that luck was when skill met necessity and that his lightning theory was worth proving. Besides, he said, we had fished in the wildness of a storm, and what better way to end a day than to be wringing the wildness out of your wet clothes, sucking the wild rain out of your cuff, thirsty for more.

What went into a boy, stayed inside. I hid it away, kept my father's voice inside me, packed in close to my heart. Whatever my father told me I always regarded as the absolute truth. I believed in the river gods. Believed that river water came from their veins; that if there was one god, He must be made entirely of water. That

109

was years ago. For years I kept lists and journals of what I remembered my father telling me. It was all good.

Take the river inside as you would a text he would tell me more than once. He knew that once inside you could memorize every pool and run, every rock in a stream and unless there was a winter of bad anchor ice, you could come back in the spring for opening day and look for every mark you'd imagined in the winter. Even better, he told me, was the ability to enter the river inside whenever you felt the need to. "I got to light out for the territory" he was fond of saying, a good part of him given over to the wildest parts of Huck Finn's personality. And always there was that dark, brooding sense of the surreal, the river looming up inside both of us as if it were alive and breathing through our skins.

But, what I remember most clearly now is the way his voice sounded on the day he died. He was barely coherent, wandering through the double stupor of morphine and the cancer in his head. He was almost dead, but you could tell his mind was still reeling with images. On this last day he was talking rivers, and trips he'd taken. I showed him a new reel and he launched himself into a beautiful story about fishing the Two-Hearted again. Then, he said he had been overtaken the night before by a dream that he had turned into something purely wild. He didn't know what it was, he said, but he knew he had moved with grace, and that he had moved under the earth with great force. He said that when he woke up, he felt a part of him was missing and that he had some sense in the dream that he had been deposited somewhere. Surely, he said, he must have dreamed himself into a river. He knew, and I remember him telling me, that there were Sioux Indians who could turn themselves into rivers. He said he had seen one such man when he was a boy travelling through Nebraska with his father. The Sioux had simply lain down, begun singing in low tones, stretching himself out further and further until he literally flowed past his feet.

My father's last dream had taken him back to that day, back to that wondrous opportunity to see flesh transcend itself. Now my father, weak from disease, lay still in his bed, only his mouth moving. What he told me on that last day was to honor my promise to take him away, to take him back to the river.

I remember my father telling me he had scouted years for the spot. He was never one for fanfare, nor ceremony, and the measure of a good day was calculated by hard work. A good spot had requirements he had said: shade most of the day, a gravel bottom and a mixture of currents, a mixing place. We visited only once. That afternoon he sat with me and talked mostly of dams. It was either a wing dam, he thought, or more probably a coffer dam.

In the sunlight that filtered through the trees he drew diagrams in the dirt. Head the river off gently, he said, or it would surge over everything. With leaves he made the wash of the river, traced it exactly over the spot where he wanted the grave. Mud he said, the trunks of trees jammed by the current against steel rods driven into the bed of the river to hold back the water. He was firm about this desire, and his firmness carried itself into the waking dreams I had of the dam, the daily visions I had of myself felling trees, driving the steel rods, packing mud like a beaver.

After he died I simply carried him off from the funeral parlor, out the back door and into the truck. His friends buried the coffin in the cemetery on the hill and I drove his body to the river.

I worked most of the first day cutting. The trees came down on the bank and I moved over their limbs as if the saw were a scythe. He lay up higher on the bank, his head on a rock like he was sleeping. I drove the stakes in two feet of water, then rolled the trees in, guiding their huge trunks against the stakes.

That night I worked against the river, my hands digging up river stones, mud, clay from the banks. I looked often at him lying up above me, his face barely visible in the cast of light from the lantern. I had made the cuts like he had instructed. Like putting a log cabin together he had motioned in the dirt that day, one log grooved, the other mortised. The seam of the logs joining together was barely a scar against my hands.

I slept off and on, working, sleeping. Packing mud and clay, repacking small spots where the water wanted to get in. When I finished I was standing in something that looked like a wooden arm growing out of the bank and angling back against the flow of the river. At the lip of the dam I held my hand against the water then turned back to look at the moist bottom of the river below me open to daylight.

I dug down below grade, through rocks and smaller rocks, into the clay that cradled the river, the water seeping into the grave.

No mumbo-jumbo he had said, no remorse, just let me go back. I laid him face up at first, then rolled him to his side so one ear might be toward the river, the other toward the sky. I packed him in, tight he had said, wedged into the bottom of the river and then I covered him, first with clay and heavy stones, then with lighter rocks and pebbles.

I waited until early evening, lit the lantern and then began dismantling the dam, only enough to let the water in, letting two logs drift away in the darkening current. The water sluiced over the dam, now inches under water, over the stones, and sifted down, I am sure into my father's lips. I wanted to speak something to him in the dark but couldn't. He had wanted silence; wanted the sound of the river all around us.

Now, in summer I drift over his spot. The remnants of the dam still hold. I imagine my father has gone back completely by now, and only his bones are held in the belly of the river. I think of him often, how he carried me far beyond the years he could. How his life merged and moved with mine and then swept in another direction. I think of him alive and casting, examining and selecting flies like a surgeon, his love of poems and wildness fused together and fueled by his desire to take in all of the world in front of him. I think of how his life comes back to me each time I fish, each time I step into the current. Mostly, I think of how both of us are carried by rivers, how his memory sifts through me like the current where only his bones are left to tell the story.

Titles in the
Great Lakes Books
Series

Freshwater Fury: Yarns and Reminiscences of the Greatest Storm in Inland Navigation, by Frank Barcus, 1986 (reprint)

Call It North Country: The Story of Upper Michigan, by John Bartlow Martin, 1986 (reprint)

The Land of the Crooked Tree, by U. P. Hedrick, 1986 (reprint)

Michigan Place Names, by Walter Romig, 1986 (reprint)

Luke Karamazov, by Conrad Hilberry, 1987

The Late, Great Lakes: An Environmental History, by William Ashworth, 1987 (reprint)

Great Pages of Michigan History from the Detroit Free Press, 1987

Waiting for the Morning Train: An American Boyhood, by Bruce Catton, 1987 (reprint)

Michigan Voices: Our State's History in the Words of the People Who Lived It, compiled and edited by Joe Grimm, 1987

Danny and the Boys, Being Some Legends of Hungry Hollow, by Robert Traver, 1987 (reprint)

Hanging On, or How to Get through a Depression and Enjoy Life, by Edmund G. Love, 1987 (reprint)

The Situation in Flushing, by Edmund G. Love, 1987 (reprint)

A Small Bequest, by Edmund G. Love, 1987 (reprint)

The Saginaw Paul Bunyan, by James Stevens, 1987 (reprint)

The Ambassador Bridge: A Monument to Progress, by Philip P. Mason, 1988

Let the Drum Beat: A History of the Detroit Light Guard, by Stanley D. Solvick, 1988

An Afternoon in Waterloo Park, by Gerald Dumas, 1988 (reprint)

Contemporary Michigan Poetry: Poems from the Third Coast, edited by Michael Delp, Conrad Hilberry and Herbert Scott, 1988

Over the Graves of Horses, by Michael Delp, 1988

Wolf in Sheep's Clothing: The Search for a Child Killer, by Tommy McIntyre, 1988

Copper-Toed Boots, by Marguerite de Angeli, 1989 (reprint)

Detroit Images: Photographs of the Renaissance City, edited by John J. Bukowczyk and Douglas Aikenhead, with Peter Slavcheff, 1989

Hangdog Reef: Poems Sailing the Great Lakes, by Stephen Tudor, 1989

Detroit: City of Race and Class Violence, revised edition, by B. J. Widick, 1989

Deep Woods Frontier: A History of Logging in Northern Michigan, by Theodore J. Karamanski, 1989

Orvie, The Dictator of Dearborn, by David L. Good, 1989

Seasons of Grace: A History of the Catholic Archdiocese of Detroit, by Leslie Woodcock Tentler, 1990

The Pottery of John Foster: Form and Meaning, by Gordon and Elizabeth Orear, 1990

The Diary of Bishop Frederic Baraga: First Bishop of Marquette, Michigan, edited by Regis M. Walling and Rev. N. Daniel Rupp, 1990

Walnut Pickles and Watermelon Cake: A Century of Michigan Cooking, by Larry B. Massie and Priscilla Massie, 1990

The Making of Michigan, 1820–1860: A Pioneer Anthology, edited by Justin L. Kestenbaum, 1990

America's Favorite Homes: A Guide to Popular Early Twentieth-Century Homes, by Robert Schweitzer and Michael W. R. Davis, 1990

Beyond the Model T: The Other Ventures of Henry Ford, by Ford R. Bryan, 1990

Life after the Line, by Josie Kearns, 1990

Michigan Lumbertowns: Lumbermen and Laborers in Saginaw, Bay City, and Muskegon, 1870–1905, by Jeremy W. Kilar, 1990

Detroit Kids Catalog: The Hometown Tourist by Ellyce Field, 1990

Waiting for the News, by Leo Litwak, 1990 (reprint)

Detroit Perspectives, edited by Wilma Wood Henrickson, 1991

Life on the Great Lakes: A Wheelsman's Story, by Fred W. Dutton, edited by William Donohue Ellis, 1991

Copper Country Journal: The Diary of Schoolmaster Henry Hobart, 1863–1864, by Henry Hobart, edited by Philip P. Mason, 1991

John Jacob Astor: Business and Finance in the Early Republic, by John Denis Haeger, 1991

Survival and Regeneration: Detroit's American Indian Community, by Edmund J. Danziger, Jr., 1991

Steamboats and Sailors of the Great Lakes, by Mark L. Thompson, 1991

Cobb Would Have Caught It: The Golden Years of Baseball in Detroit, by Richard Bak, 1991

Michigan in Literature, by Clarence Andrews, 1992

Under the Influence of Water: Poems, Essays, and Stories, by Michael Delp, 1992

The Country Kitchen, by Della T. Lutes, 1992 (reprint)

The Making of a Mining District: Keweenaw Native Copper 1500–1870, by David J. Krause, 1992

Kids Catalog of Michigan Adventures, by Ellyce Field, 1993

Henry's Lieutenants, by Ford R. Bryan, 1993

Historic Highway Bridges of Michigan, by Charles K. Hyde, 1993

Lake Erie and Lake St. Clair Handbook, by Stanley J. Bolsenga and Charles E. Herndendorf, 1993

Queen of the Lakes, by Mark Thompson, 1994

Iron Fleet: The Great Lakes in World War II, by George J. Joachim, 1994

Turkey Stearnes and the Detroit Stars: The Negro Leagues in Detroit, 1919–1933, by Richard Bak, 1994

Pontiac and the Indian Uprising, by Howard H. Peckham, 1994 (reprint)

Charting the Inland Seas: A History of the U.S. Lake Survey, by Arthur M. Woodford, 1994 (reprint)

Ojibwa Narratives of Charles and Charlotte Kawbawgam and Jacques LePique, 1893–1895. Recorded with Notes by Homer H. Kidder, edited by Arthur P. Bourgeois, 1994, co-published with the Marquette County Historical Society

Strangers and Sojourners: A History of Michigan's Keweenaw Peninsula, by Arthur W. Thurner, 1994

Win Some, Lose Some: G. Mennen Williams and the New Democrats, by Helen Washburn Berthelot, 1995

Sarkis, by Gordon and Elizabeth Orear, 1995

The Northern Lights: Lighthouses of the Upper Great Lakes, by Charles K. Hyde, 1995 (reprint)

Kids Catalog of Michigan Adventures, second edition, by Ellyce Field, 1995

Rumrunning and the Roaring Twenties: Prohibition on the Michigan–Ontario Waterway, by Philip P. Mason, 1995

In the Wilderness with the Red Indians, by E. R. Baierlein, translated by Anita Z. Boldt, edited by Harold W. Moll, 1996

Elmwood Endures: History of a Detroit Cemetery, by Michael Franck, 1996

Master of Precision: Henry M. Leland, by Mrs. Wilfred C. Leland with Minnie Dubbs Millbrook, 1996 (reprint)

Haul-Out: New and Selected Poems, by Stephen Tudor, 1996

Kids Catalog of Michigan Adventures, third edition, by Ellyce Field, 1997

Beyond the Model T: The Other Ventures of Henry Ford, revised edition, by Ford R. Bryan, 1997

Young Henry Ford: A Picture History of the First Forty Years, by Sidney Olson, 1997 (reprint)

These Men Have Seen Hard Service: The First Michigan Sharpshooters in the Civil War, by Raymond J. Herek, 1997

The Coast of Nowhere: Meditations on Rivers, Lakes and Streams, by Michael Delp, 1997

From Saginaw Valley to Tin Pan Alley: Saginaw's Contribution to American Popular Music, 1890–1955, by R. Grant Smith, 1997

Toast of the Town: The Life and Times of Sunnie Wilson, by Sunnie Wilson with John Cohassey, 1997

The Long Winter Ends, by Newton George Thomas, 1997 (reprint)

Bridging the River of Hatred: The Pioneering Efforts of Detroit Police Commissioner George Edwards, 1962–1963, by Mary M. Stolberg, 1998

A Place for Summer: One Hundred Years at Michigan and Trumbull, by Richard Bak, 1998

Michigan in the Novel, 1816–1996: An Annotated Bibliography, by Robert Beasecker, 1998